Body Awareness

by Annie Baker

SAMUEL FRENCH

FOUNDED 1830

NEW YORK HOLLYWOOD LONDON TORONTO

SAMUELFRENCH.COM

ISBN 978-0-573-66310-9   Printed in U.S.A.   #4254

000216865

IMPORTANT BILLING AND CREDIT REQUIREMENTS

All producers of *BODY AWARENESS must* give credit to the Author of the Play in all programs distributed in connection with performances of the Play, and in all instances in which the title of the Play appears for the purposes of advertising, publicizing or otherwise exploiting the Play and/or a production. The name of the Author *must* appear on a separate line on which no other name appears, immediately following the title and *must* appear in size of type not less than fifty percent of the size of the title type.

In addition the following credit must be given in all programs and publicity information distributed in association with this piece:

BODY AWARENESS was developed at the 2007 Bay Area Playwrights Festival, a program of the Playwrights Foundation, Amy L. Mueller, Artistic Director

World Premiere
Presented by
Atlantic Theatre Company
New York City, 2008

ATLANTIC THEATER COMPANY

Neil Pepe
Artistic Director

Mary McCann
School Executive Director

Andrew D. Hamingson
Managing Director

presents

AWARENESS

by
Annie Baker

with

Jonathan Clem, Peter Friedman,
Mary McCann, JoBeth Williams

sets
Walt Spangler

costumes
Bobby Frederick Tilley II

lights
Jason Lyons

sound
Anthony Gabriele

casting
MelCap Casting

production stage manager
Jillian M. Oliver

assistant stage manager
John Randolph Ferry

production manager
Gabriel Evansohn

general manager
Jamie Tyrol

associate artistic director
Christian Parker

press representative
Boneau/Bryan-Brown

directed by
Karen Kohlhaas

Body Awareness was developed at the 2007 Bay Area Playwrights Festival, a program of the
Playwrights Foundation, Amy L. Mueller, Artistic Director

We are grateful for the support of Atlantic Stage 2 from: The Lila Acheson Wallace Theater Fund / The
Educational Foundation of America / The John Golden Fund / The Blanche and Irving Laurie
Foundation / The Lucille Lortel Foundation / Time Warner, Inc

This program is supported, in part, by public funds from the New York City Department of Cultural Affairs.

This project is supported, in part, by an award from the National Endowment for the Arts.

CHARACTERS

JOYCE - 55
JARED - 21, her son
PHYLLIS - 45, her girlfriend
FRANK BONITATIBUS - 59

SET

Stage left is Joyce and Phyllis's kitchen. There's a sink and a stove, a table with chairs, and a bookshelf with a multi-volume set of the OED.

Center stage is a queen-sized bed. This is Joyce and Phyllis's bedroom.

Stage right is a blackboard.

The characters should wander freely in and out of the sets during the scene transitions, turning on lights, removing props, etc.

AUTHOR'S NOTE

BODY AWARENESS should be played as naturalistically as possible. Forget that it's a comedy. I've found that the play works best (and is actually funnier) when everything is played in earnest, and everyone stops worrying about getting the audience to laugh.

Feel free to draw out the pauses, and make them really agonizing.

This play is dedicated to Linda Baker

(Lights up on **PHYLLIS** *standing in front of the black-board, clutching a microphone and a few index cards. She is nervous. Written across the blackboard is the word "Monday".* **PHYLLIS** *takes a deep breath.)*

PHYLLIS. The goal for Body Awareness Week is threefold.

(pause)

One: it's a catalyst for discussion.

Two: it's a chance for everyone here at Shirley State to just kind of *check in*: first with ourselves, and our own bodies, and then with our thoughts and judgments about other people's bodies. We live in a very harsh culture, a culture that encourages a real obsession with appearance, and, um, healing from this culture, healing ourselves, can only really take place once we're able to step back and examine the culture itself from a critical viewpoint. Deepak Chopra uses a, what I think is a really great example of flies stuck in a jar: if you keep the lid on for long enough, when you finally take it off, only a few flies are actually brave enough to leave the, ah, *confines* of the jar. The rest just keep flying around inside.

(she takes a deep breath)

Three: we've invited some really fabulous guest artists to campus this week, so it's a great opportunity for all of us to really look at art in a new way. I mean, if you think about it, so *much* of art is about body awareness, or at least gaze awareness...so faculty members, if any of this is applicable to your class work...don't make it a source of stress or anything, but there is just *so much* potential discussion surrounding these issues.

(after a pause, peering out)

Wow. It's really snowing out there.

(she smiles nervously)

I guess that's it. It's Monday! We've got five very eventful days ahead of us. I'm, ah...I'm really excited about this.

*(Blackout on **PHYLLIS**.)*

*(**JOYCE** and **PHYLLIS**'s kitchen. **JOYCE** and **JARED** sit at the table. **JARED** wears his McDonald's uniform. After a long silence:)*

JOYCE. We're fine with you masturbating, Jared.

*(**JARED** does not respond.)*

JOYCE. This is not about the fact that you masturbate.

(another silence)

The thing is...you can't rack up those charges. We see them on the bill.

JARED. Okay.

JOYCE. You're free to use the internet, or purchase whatever yourself...

(another awkward pause)

...We just can't afford the Pay-Per-View.

JARED. This is really gross.

JOYCE. What's gross?

JARED. Talking about this.

JOYCE. Yeah, well, I think women with no body hair? I think that's gross.

*(**JARED** is silent.)*

JOYCE. You know people don't really look like that, right? It will be extremely hard for you to find a real person who looks like that.

*(**JARED** refuses to look at her.)*

JOYCE. Those women have had extensive plastic surgery and really painful hair waxing procedures. I assume you know that we all have pubic hair for a reason.

(a long pause)

What are you thinking about?

JARED. Why do you care?

JOYCE. I love you…? I think you're fabulous…?

JARED. OED stuff.

JOYCE. Any specific word?

JARED. I was thinking about the definition for "imbecile."

JOYCE. That sounds like a fun one.

(*JARED gazes at her suspiciously, then continues.*)

JARED. Nowadays "imbecile" just means someone stupid. But it used to mean "physically weak." It originally comes from the Latin for "without a supporting staff."

JOYCE. Huh.

JARED. What's weird is that this implies there was a time when "physically weak" and "stupid" were synonymous.

JOYCE. Yeah. I avoid using the word "stupid" whenever possible. It's kind of judgmental, don't you think?

(*JARED abruptly stands up, takes a book out of his backpack, and puts it down on the table.*)

JOYCE. Wow. You read the whole thing?

JARED. Yes. Well. I perused it.

JOYCE. And?

JARED. It was extremely well-written.

JOYCE. It's a fast read, right?

JARED. I don't really care about whether something is a "fast read."

JOYCE. No, I just meant…Phyllis says he's an incredible psychologist. Like, renowned.

(*A pause.*)

JOYCE.	JARED.
Do you think –	I don't have it.

JOYCE. …Okay. We don't need to jump to any conclusions right now. I…Phyllis and I just wanted you to think about it, and then –

JARED. I can tell you with 100 percent certainty that I don't have it.

JOYCE. That's great. That's great.

(after a pause)

I just think that if we all went and met with a psychologist he or she could give us a more definite –

JARED. I AM NOT FUCKING RETARDED.

JOYCE. Tone Of Voice.

JARED. I am not fucking retarded.

JOYCE.	**JARED.**
It doesn't mean you're retarded. It's a social –	I don't have it.

JARED. They give that example. If an Asperger's person walks in the front door and sees a loved one crying they don't stop and ask What's Wrong?

JOYCE. Uh huh.

JARED. I can say with 100 percent certainty that I would stop and ask What's Wrong.

JOYCE. Really? The last time you saw me crying you told me to stop and make you a snack.

JARED. You were crying for a stupid reason.

JOYCE. I was crying because you threatened to stab me in the eye.

JARED. I just…I'm obviously a really smart person.

JOYCE. It doesn't mean you're not smart. It just means you have trouble relating to people.

(JARED picks up his backpack.)

JARED. I have to go to work.

JOYCE. I love you. Hey. Don't forget. Our guest artist is coming tomorrow. So keep things neat.

JARED. Is it a man?

JOYCE. I don't know.

JARED. I would prefer that it not be a man.

JOYCE. I really don't have any control over that, sweet-heart.

(JARED walks out of the room. After a few seconds, he walks back in.)

JARED. Maybe you have Asperger's.

JOYCE. Jared.

JARED. Because you're kind of an idiot.

JOYCE. I'm not an idiot, honey.

JARED. You've never read "Crime and Punishment." You're fifty-five and you've never read "Crime and Punishment."

JOYCE. Have *you* ever read "Crime and Punishment"?

(**JARED** *roars in frustration and takes an electric tooth-brush out of his pocket. He turns it on and starts passing the toothbrush back and forth between his hands.* **JOYCE** *watches him.*)

JOYCE. If you're angry at me just say it. You don't have to insult me. You can say: I'm feeling really angry right now, Mom.

JARED. I'm not angry. I'm surrounded by imbeciles. You don't even…you don't even read the dictionary!

JOYCE. You're going to be late.

(**JARED** *stops and stares at her, seething with rage.*)

JARED. I could kill you.

JOYCE. Warning One.

JARED. I could kill Phyllis.

JOYCE. Warning Two.

JARED. I could garrote both of you in your sleep.

JOYCE. …Warning Three. If you make one more physical threat I will call the police.

JARED. I have First Amendment Rights.

JOYCE. You are not allowed to physically threaten people and you know that.

JARED. First Amendment says I can physically threaten people.

JOYCE. No it doesn't.

JARED. Yes it does.

JOYCE. No. It doesn't.

JARED. BABBLING CRETIN!

(*JOYCE collapses onto the table and buries her face in her arms. It's unclear whether or not she's crying.* **JARED** *stands there and watches her for a while. He turns off the toothbrush.*)

JARED. I won't kill you.

(*Silence.*)

JARED. I was joking.

(*Silence.*)

JARED. What's wrong?

(**JOYCE** *does not respond.*)

JARED. See? I asked.

(*Blackout.*)

(**JOYCE** *and* **PHYLLIS**'*s bedroom.* **JOYCE** *and* **PHYLLIS** *sit up in bed together, lit by the bedside lamp.* **PHYLLIS** *is reading the Asperger's book.* **JOYCE** *is clipping her toenails and depositing them on the nightstand.*)

JOYCE. There's this weird *crud* all over my toenails.

PHYLLIS. (*not looking up from her book*) What color is it?

JOYCE. Gray-ish?

PHYLLIS. Ew.

(*After a pause,* **PHYLLIS** *puts down the book.*)

PHYLLIS. If he doesn't think he has it how does he explain the fact that he still lives with his mother?

JOYCE. There are lots of cultures where children live with their parents through adulthood.

PHYLLIS. And rack up porn bills?

JOYCE. America is very strange. We're so focused on independence. It's like, you can't need anybody. You have to be this totally autonomous…*person.*

PHYLLIS. Hey. Speaking of other cultures. I finally met the Palestinian Dance Troupe kids.

JOYCE. Oh! Cute!

PHYLLIS. They were amazing. They've been living in these

refugee camps since they were babies? And they were
/all –

JOYCE. Wait. I don't get it. How do they relate to Body
Awareness?

PHYLLIS. Well. They're a dance troupe. For one thing.

JOYCE. Huh.

PHYLLIS. And they're very political.

JOYCE. Right.

(**JOYCE** *goes back to clipping her toenails.*)

PHYLLIS. Hey. My eye is twitching. Can you tell?

(**JOYCE** *looks at her.*)

JOYCE. Where?

PHYLLIS. Left one.

JOYCE. Nope.

PHYLLIS. I can feel it, um…it's sort of pulsing? Just like this
little pulsing –

JOYCE. I don't see anything.

(**JARED** *yells from offstage:*)

JARED. *(O.S.)* I CAN HEAR YOU GUYS TALKING AND I'M
ATTEMPTING TO FALL ASLEEP!

(**PHYLLIS** *and* **JOYCE** *look at each other, amused.*)

JARED. *(O.S.)* I HAVE TO GET UP AT SIX IN THE MORN-
ING!

JOYCE. *(calling out)* Okay, okay, we hear you!

JARED. *(O.S.)* I ACTUALLY HAVE A JOB!

PHYLLIS. *(yelling back good-naturedly)* We have jobs too!

JARED. *(O.S.)* IN ACADEMIA!

PHYLLIS. *(laughing)* YOUR MOTHER'S JOB DOES NOT
COUNT AS ACADEMIA!

(**PHYLLIS** *grins at* **JOYCE**. **JOYCE** *stares at her for a few
seconds, then:*)

JOYCE. What do you mean, it doesn't count as academia?

PHYLLIS. A high school teacher is not an academic.

JOYCE. Why not?

PHYLLIS. An academic has a PhD.

JOYCE. Who says?

PHYLLIS. Um. It's common knowledge?

JOYCE. I've never heard that before.

PHYLLIS. Joyce. A public school teacher is not an academic. An academic publishes articles. An academic –

JOYCE. You are such a snob.

PHYLLIS. What? No. I'm the *opposite* of a snob. How am I a snob?

JARED. *(O.S.)* WILL BOTH OF YOU KINDLY CEASE SPEAKING!

(**PHYLLIS** *and* **JOYCE** *fall silent. After a short pause, the buzzing sound of the electric toothbrush is heard from offstage.*)

PHYLLIS. *(softly)* Oh please. He's not sleeping. He's sticking his toothbrush up his ass.

JOYCE. Phil.

PHYLLIS. What?

JOYCE. He likes rubbing it against his gums. He finds it soothing.

(**PHYLLIS** *holds up the Asperger's book.*)

PHYLLIS. Did you read the part where it says that they get really dependant on certain objects and rituals?

JOYCE. Yeah.

PHYLLIS. Also they have an unbelievably sensitive sense of smell. *Totally* Jared.

(after a pause)

I can't get over the fact that you never made him see a therapist.

JOYCE. He refuses to go.

PHYLLIS. Yeah, but with certain kids you just have insist / on –

JOYCE. *(defensively)* For a while it seemed like he was gonna be fine.

(PHYLLIS sighs.)

JOYCE. For a while it seemed that way!

PHYLLIS. I'm gonna turn off the light.

JOYCE. He had friends in elementary school. This little clique of boys?

(PHYLLIS reaches over and turns off the lamp. They're barely visible in the moonlight. After a pause, quietly, out of the darkness:)

JOYCE. He was a *very* cuddly baby.

PHYLLIS. Okay, okay.

(A pause.)

JOYCE. Will you spoon me?

PHYLLIS. Mmm.

(The sound of sheets rustling. They settle into a comfortable position. After a few seconds:)

JOYCE. God. I can't stop thinking about this girl in my B period class. Loreen? I told you about her.

PHYLLIS. I'm really tired, sweetheart.

JOYCE. She's so *makeup-y*. I don't know. It's weird. There's something really nervous and sexualized about her.

PHYLLIS. Mmhm.

JOYCE. I think maybe she was molested.

PHYLLIS. You think everyone was molested.

JOYCE. Well, 1 out of 4 /women –

PHYLLIS. Yeah, but you think EVERYONE was molested.

JOYCE. That's not true.

PHYLLIS. You thought I was molested. When you met me.

JOYCE. Well, you seemed kind of…molested.

(after a long pause)

Will you do it again?

PHYLLIS. Oh my god. I'm so tired.

(There is a rustling underneath the covers.)

JOYCE. Higher.

(after a pause)

Yeah. There.

PHYLLIS. Okay.

JOYCE. Is that weird?

PHYLLIS. Yeah, Joyce.

JOYCE. Is that thigh? Or is it crotch?

(after a long silence)

Is it weird for someone to put their –

PHYLLIS. It's weird.

JOYCE. It could have been nothing.

PHYLLIS. It's weird, honey.

JOYCE. He could have just…

(JOYCE *trails off.)*

PHYLLIS. Your father was *definitely* a bastard. Can we go to sleep?

JOYCE. Yeah. Yeah. Sorry.

(The two women shift around in bed and embrace each other. Slowly, morning light comes through the window.)

(PHYLLIS *gets up out of bed and walks over to the blackboard. She writes "Tuesday" on the board, then turns to the audience and speaks into a microphone.)*

PHYLLIS. It's an honor just to stand here and introduce the next performers. They've flown across oceans, and, um, continents to perform for us, and they're an unbelievably strong, brave group of children. People. They came together in a refugee camp in Palestine, where, well…the word that comes to my mind is "hopelessness." In a place of hopelessness they formed a community, and they created this work of dance… it's pretty mind-blowing. So without further ado –

(she hesitates)

Oh. Sorry. One more thing. Just a nomenclature issue. This week, um, February 20th to the 27th, is, offi-cially, National Eating Disorder Awareness Week. But

I wanted to reiterate that here at Shirley State College we've chosen to call it Body Awareness Week. There's still gonna be the roundtable discussion on eating disorders, but we feel it's important to take a more positive tack and make the whole thing about the larger issue of Self Image in general. And this way we get to see incredible groups like Idbaal perform! So just a reminder, it's not Eating Disorder Awareness Week at Shirley State, it's *Body Awareness* Week. If we could correct the mistake on any posters or publicity materials, that would be great. Okay. Prepare to be...very moved. I'd like to welcome Idbaal!

(She steps aside. Pounding Palestinian music starts playing. Blackout.)

(JOYCE *and* **PHYLLIS** *'s kitchen.* **FRANK BONITATIBUS** *stands in the middle of the kitchen, playing the recorder.* **JOYCE** *is sitting at the table and watching him, utterly enchanted. He finishes, lowers the recorder and smiles at her. After a pause:)*

JOYCE. Oh. My. God.

FRANK. You enjoyed it?

JOYCE. That was *otherworldly.*

FRANK. Mmm.

(They grin at each other for a while. Finally **JOYCE** *shakes her head, as if to clear her thoughts.)*

JOYCE. I should start making dinner.

(JOYCE *gets up from the table and starts getting vegetables out of the fridge.* **FRANK** *trails her around the kitchen while she prepares the meal. He continually munches from a bowl of baby carrots on the kitchen table.)*

FRANK. So you teach high school?

JOYCE. Yup.

FRANK. What do you teach?

JOYCE. Cultural Studies.

FRANK. Is that like Social Studies?

JOYCE. It's a little different.

FRANK. How?

JOYCE. Um, well, we sort of take more of an anthropological perspective?

(She starts cutting up the vegetables. **FRANK** *peers at some of the pictures on the refrigerator.)*

FRANK. How long have you and your girlfriend been together?

JOYCE. Three years.

FRANK. Wow. Great.

JOYCE. It is great.

FRANK. Do you call her that? Your girlfriend? Is it okay? To call her that?

JOYCE. Um, well, some people –

FRANK. Do you prefer "partner" or something?

JOYCE. Oh. I don't know. Well, actually, /yes. I –

FRANK. "Partner" sounds so DIPPY, though. You know what I mean?

JOYCE. Um –

FRANK. Have you always been… ?

*(**FRANK** makes a vague gesture.)*

JOYCE. Uh. No. I have a son. You'll meet him. Yeah. I was married. To a man. Years ago. Phyllis was actually my first, um, female partner.

FRANK. What about her?

JOYCE. Oh, Phyllis. Yeah. Phyllis knew she was gay when she was in kindergarten.

FRANK. Three years together. Huh.

(after a pause)

You really feel like you know each other after three years.

*(**JOYCE** nods.)*

But then one day the person says something really weird and you're like: DO I actually know you? Or are you this total stranger?

(**JOYCE** *doesn't respond. She finishes chopping vegetables and starts putting them into a pot on the stove.*)

FRANK. Anyway.

JOYCE. Are you in a relationship?

FRANK. No. I'm actually incredibly happy to be single. Just taking stock of things.

(**JOYCE** *nods.*)

You live here. That's so strange.

(**JOYCE** *nods again.*)

"Shirley, Vermont." This is a weird town.

JOYCE. It's small.

FRANK. Yeah. Small and weird.

(**JOYCE** *starts stirring and seasoning.*)

Is everyone really P.C.? Are people like, don't say "black person," say "person of color"?

JOYCE. Oh. Well. I don't know. I /think –

FRANK. Don't say "retarded," say "mentally disabled"?

JOYCE. Actually –

FRANK. People in towns like this always seem to find my work threatening.

JOYCE. But your pictures are so moving!

FRANK. It's like you're not allowed to do anything involving naked women anymore. If a woman is naked, you're a misogynist.

JOYCE. But you have so many *types* of women –

FRANK. I know –

JOYCE. – that one photo of the old lady? With the mastectomy?

FRANK. Yeah.

JOYCE. It was gorgeous. The way she was smiling?

(*The buzzing sound of* **JARED***'s toothbrush is heard from offstage.*)

FRANK. Do you hear that?

JOYCE. My son must be home.

FRANK. Yeah, but what's that sound?

(**JOYCE** *hesitates.*)

JOYCE. Um. You should probably know. Jared is kind of... special.

(**FRANK** *looks at her.*)

FRANK. Special meaning what?

JOYCE. Um. I think he has something called Asperger's? I'd like him to see a therapist about it. He refuses to, / but –

FRANK. I've heard of that. It's like lack of empathy, right?

JOYCE. There are less negative ways to put it.

FRANK. No, I just –

JOYCE. There's this thing called Theory of Mind? It's our ability to know that other people don't know what we're thinking...that we each have these independent mental states? People with Aspberger's have a hard time –

(**JARED** *enters the kitchen, sucking on his toothbrush.*)

JARED. The whole house smells like meatloaf.

JOYCE. No one's making meatloaf.

JARED. It smells like meatloaf.

JOYCE. Jared. This is Frank Bonitatibus.

(**FRANK** *extends his hand.* **JARED** *lifts his hand up in a limp salute, but doesn't touch* **FRANK**. *After a second, he turns off the toothbrush.*)

JARED. I don't have Asperger's.

JOYCE. You were eavesdropping.

JARED. Stop telling everyone I'm retarded.

JOYCE. I never said you were retarded.

JARED. *(to* **FRANK***)* She made me take classes with the retarded kids in high school.

JOYCE. I made you take one Organizational Skills class.

JARED. *(to* **FRANK***)* I'm incredibly smart –

FRANK. *(nervously)* Of course –

JARED. – and she made me take this class with the Special Ed kids. This one guy kept going like this:

(he bobbles his head back and forth)

"You owe me three dollah. You owe me three dollah."

(**JARED** *starts laughing.*)

JOYCE. Okay. Enough.

FRANK. Are you a student at Shirley State?

JARED. College is stupid. Buncha frat girls and guys having sex with each other.

FRANK. That's not what my college experience was like.

JARED. People do drugs and go to parties.

FRANK. Where is he getting this stuff?

JOYCE. I don't know. I told him how much I loved Brandeis.

JARED. It doesn't really matter anyway. I'm an autodidact.

FRANK. Oh yeah?

JARED. Do you know what that means?

FRANK. I think so.

JARED. It comes from the Greek.

FRANK. You know Greek?

JARED. I know etymology.

FRANK. What's that?

JARED. Ha.

(to **JOYCE***)*

He doesn't know what etymology means.

JOYCE. It's a big word, Jared.

FRANK. Wait. I think I know what it means. The beginning of things? /The –

JARED. WRONG.

JOYCE. Why don't you tell him?

FRANK. I don't need him to tell me.

JARED. The origins and histories of words.

FRANK. Sure. Of course.

JARED. It's my strength. It's proof that I'm not a retard.

JOYCE. Please stop saying retard.

FRANK. *(to JARED)* You ever seen "Rain Man"?

JARED. No.

FRANK. Dustin Hoffman is this retarded guy, but he's like a genius in certain subjects. He's always freaking out and doing these little flappy –

JOYCE. *(getting upset)* That's autism. I think you're talking about autism. Jared has Asperger's. It's on the autism spectrum, but it's actually a much milder –

JARED. I DON'T HAVE IT. FUCKING SHIT!

> *(FRANK looks at JOYCE, expecting her to say something. JOYCE goes back to stirring the soup.)*

FRANK. *(to JARED)* Uh…if you don't go to college what do you do?

JARED. Lots of things. I'm an autodidact.

JOYCE. I think he means where do you work.

JARED. I work at McDonald's.

FRANK. Oh, hey, good, great. Hard-workin' man!

JARED. Everyone there is an idiot.

FRANK. I'm sure that's not true.

JARED. It smells like meatloaf in here. Also like glitter. That glue and glitter smell?

> *(JOYCE ignores him. JARED takes a volume of the OED off of the bookshelf, sits down at the kitchen table, and starts reading it.)*

FRANK. This is an interesting family.

JOYCE. Mmm. We're very open.

> *(PHYLLIS enters through the backdoor.)*

JOYCE. Phil! This is our guest artist!

PHYLLIS. Hey! Oh great! I'm Phyllis. I'm one of the, ah, many organizers.

> *(They shake hands.)*

FRANK. Frank Bonitatibus. It's incredibly generous of you to let me –

PHYLLIS. Oh, no! Please. Thank *you.*

(**PHYLLIS** *beams happily at him, then walks over to* **JOYCE** *and kisses her.*)

PHYLLIS. Hey, ladybug.

FRANK. *(inserting himself back into the conversation)* …It's just so nice to stay in an actual *house.* Usually I just end up sitting alone in a hotel room and drinking beer.

PHYLLIS. We don't drink in this house.

FRANK. No, that's fine, that's not /what –

JARED. *(looking up from his book)* Yes we do. We drink milk. We drink water.

PHYLLIS. I mean alcohol, Jared.

JARED. We drink Cranberry Raspberry Cocktail.

FRANK. *(nervously)* Sounds fine, sounds fine.

JARED. We drink our own urine.

(a horrible pause)

Just kidding.

FRANK. Great.

JARED. I was being ironic.

(to **FRANK***)*

The book said people with Asperger's don't know how to be ironic.

PHYLLIS. What's your medium, Frank?

FRANK. I'm a photographer.

PHYLLIS. Oh! Wonderful! I've just been working with the performance artists, /so –

JARED. Do you make daguerreotypes?

FRANK. Ah. No.

JARED. Do you know what a daguerreotype is?

FRANK. Yes.

JARED. Do you know the etymology of daguerreotype?

FRANK. No. I –

JOYCE. *(pointedly ignoring* **JARED***)* Tell Phyllis about your photographs.

(to **PHYLLIS***)*

I saw them this afternoon. They're amazing.

FRANK. Uh. Well. I take pictures of women.

JOYCE. *(giggling)* Naked women.

*(***PHYLLIS** *looks at* **JOYCE***, confused.)*

PHYLLIS. I'm sorry – ?

JOYCE. They're actually incredibly moving. You have to see it. Everyone was /just –

PHYLLIS. *(ignoring* **JOYCE***, to* **FRANK***)* Wait, why? Why do you take pictures of naked women?

FRANK. Why does anyone take pictures of anything?

JOYCE. Explain it her. It's actually wonderful.

(to **PHYLLIS***)*

He goes around –

FRANK. I go around the country. I don't pay anyone. Women volunteer to pose for me. It's a way for them to, uh, reclaim their own body image.

PHYLLIS. Why don't men pose for you?

JOYCE. It's not just, like, model types. He takes pictures of old women, little girls –

PHYLLIS. Excuse me?

FRANK. With parental permission.

(A pause.)

JARED. The word "daguerreotype" actually comes from the French inventor of the daguerreotype himself. Louis Daguerre.

PHYLLIS. Sorry. I just –

JOYCE. Phyllis is very sensitive.

PHYLLIS. Um, I don't think I'm that sensitive, Joyce. You're the one who's, like, the language police.

(An awkward pause.)

JOYCE. You know, Sally Humphries loves his stuff. She's really crazy about it.

PHYLLIS. Uh huh.

JOYCE. *(to* **FRANK***)* Phyllis was on the search committee that brought Sally Humphries into the psychology department. It was such a white-male-dominated little boy's club, and Sally is this like fabulous *fiery* African-American woman. She's actually part Native-American, too, I think...

FRANK. Oh yeah?

JOYCE. ...and she's just fabulous.

(A defeated pause.)

PHYLLIS. *(to* **FRANK***)* How do you know it isn't just exhibitionist? Or exploitative?

FRANK. It's neither.

PHYLLIS. How do you know?

FRANK. Because I'm not exploiting them, and they don't do it for exhibitionist reasons.

PHYLLIS. *(trying to sound light-hearted)* Well, I'm not posing for you.

FRANK. Don't worry, honey. I'm not asking.

PHYLLIS. Did you just call me "honey"?

JARED. *(looking up from the OED)* I refuse to get naked in front of anyone.

PHYLLIS. Frank wouldn't be interested anyway, Jared, because you're a man.

JARED. I don't want anyone to see me naked. Even if I get a girlfriend. I don't want her to look at me.

*(***JARED*** goes back to reading.)*

JOYCE. *(after an awkward pause)* Okay! Let's eat! I made this great winter soup.

JARED. It smells like meatloaf.

JOYCE. Please try to be polite. We have a guest.

(Everyone sits down at the table.)

JOYCE. *(to* **JARED***)* Can you put that away?

(JARED *puts the OED volume on his chair and sits on it.*
He's perched about five inches higher than everyone else.
JOYCE *ladles out soup.*)

FRANK. Sorry. Do you all say grace?

PHYLLIS. We're not religious.

JOYCE. I'm actually Jewish. Well. I'm half-Jewish. Phyllis /
is –

FRANK. Fantastic. That's so great.

JOYCE. But I'm not observant.

FRANK. No, that's wonderful! Jews are wonderful. My parents are Greek.

JOYCE. Very nice!

FRANK. ...But I personally take a sort of non-religious Bud-
dhist view of things. Still. Judaism is so beautiful. It's
such a dialectical religion, you know?

JARED. I never got a Bar Mitzvah.

JOYCE. He just wanted one so people would give him
money. I thought that probably wasn't the right reason
to go through with it.

FRANK. Hey. You know what? We should do a Shabbas.

JOYCE. Oh. Um. We don't really do that kind of thing.

PHYLLIS. Also it's not Friday.

FRANK. It would be such a treat for me.

JARED. Religion is stupid.

JOYCE. Jared! That's a close-minded thing to say.

FRANK. Come on.

JOYCE. It's a little embarrassing. I just...I don't think I even
know how to do Shabbas.

PHYLLIS. Why is that embarrassing?

FRANK. Ah ha. See, I do. You got any red wine?

PHYLLIS. We don't drink.

JOYCE. We have grape juice...

FRANK. Perfect.

PHYLLIS. Sorry. I...um...no one else thinks that doing
Shabbas on a Tuesday is a little disrespectful? Possibly
sacrilegious?

(JOYCE gets some grape juice out of the cupboard and puts it on the table. She gets out four wine glasses.)

JARED. Booze. Goody.

(He laughs.)

PHYLLIS. I don't want any.

JOYCE. Oh, come on.

*(She grins happily at **PHYLLIS.** **PHYLLIS** shakes her head. **JOYCE** pours her a glass of grape juice.)*

FRANK. Okay. Now sit. Please.

*(JOYCE sits. **FRANK** takes his recorder out of his pocket and plays an "A." **PHYLLIS** looks on in disbelief. **FRANK** puts his recorder back in his pocket, takes a deep breath, and closes his eyes.)*

FRANK. *(singing)* Baruch ata adonoi

eluhaynu melech hahlom

borey pree hagofen.

*(**FRANK** opens his eyes and smiles serenely.)*

FRANK. That was the prayer for wine.

PHYLLIS. How do you know the prayer for wine?

FRANK. I was married to a Jew for ten years.

JOYCE. Me too!

*(He and **JOYCE** burst into giggles. **PHYLLIS** and **JARED** are unamused.)*

PHYLLIS. Why is that funny?

JOYCE. *(ignoring her, to **FRANK**)* That was gorgeous. Thank you.

FRANK. It's not over. Do you have any candles?

JOYCE. I actually do!

(JOYCE gets up and gets out two candles and two candle-sticks. She puts them on the table.)

PHYLLIS. This is great. A goy teaching a Jew how to do Shabbas. On a Tuesday.

FRANK. I hope I'm not being presumptuous.

JOYCE. No, no. Not at all.

FRANK. Okay. Light the candles.

(**JOYCE** *lights the candles.*)

FRANK. Wave your hands around.

(**JOYCE** *jiggles her hands.*)

FRANK. No, like you're bringing the heat towards you.

(*He mimes. She obeys.*)

FRANK. Good.

JOYCE. Oh yeah! It's like that scene from "Fiddler on the Roof"!

JARED. I hate musicals.

FRANK. Now put your hands over your eyes.

(**JOYCE** *puts her hands over her eyes.* **FRANK** *takes out his recorder, gives himself another "A," and then sings the following in a pleasant monotone:*)

FRANK. Baruch atah adonai
eloheinu melech ha-olam…

JARED. You said that before.

FRANK. …this one is different…
Asher kid-shanu
b'mitzvotav v'tzivanu
l'had'like neir shel shabbat. Amein.

(*a pause*)

FRANK. (*softly*) Can we all sing that last word together?

PHYLLIS (*reluctantly*)/**JOYCE**/**FRANK.** A-a-a-a-mein.

FRANK. Now take your hands away.

(**JOYCE** *takes her hands away. They all look at her.*)

PHYLLIS. You're crying. Jesus Christ.

JOYCE. It's just…

(*to* **FRANK**)

Thank you.

(*she sits down, shakily*)

My Bubbie used to sing like that.

PHYLLIS. You were raised by atheists.

JOYCE. Not my parents. My Bubbie.

FRANK. It's nice, right? Connecting with your roots.

JARED. This soup is not as gross as I thought it would be.

JOYCE. I really love listening to people sing. Phyllis never sings. She's too self-conscious.

(PHYLLIS *stares at* JOYCE, *hurt.*)

JOYCE. What? It's true.

FRANK. Singing is very meditative.

JOYCE. *(nodding)* I wish I meditated more.

FRANK. We're all so *wound-up* all the time.

JOYCE. Exactly.

FRANK. We, uh...we walk around in these little circles, and we forget to pay attention to what we could see if we just stopped using our brains so much.

PHYLLIS. Sorry...I'm a little confused. What do you mean /by –

FRANK. There's a lot of stuff happening around us. Stuff we're not aware of most of the time. You know what I mean. We don't live in this perfectly linear universe.

PHYLLIS. I actually have no idea what you're talking about.

JOYCE. Do you mean thoughts and dreams? Or...

FRANK. Sure. Both. Also visions. Visitations.

(after a pause)

If you make yourself open.

JARED. You sound dumb.

JOYCE. Jared.

FRANK. I don't think I sound dumb.

PHYLLIS. *(to* JOYCE*)* The soup is great.

JOYCE. Thanks.

PHYLLIS. The squash is so, um –

FRANK. When I was eight I was hit by a car. I had to wear a body cast for ten months.

JOYCE. Oh my god.

FRANK. Funny things happen when you're stuck in bed for that long. I'd wake up after a nap and there would be dozen people standing around my bed. Old-fashioned people. With the big hats? Men in suits. Women with those little frilly umbrellas. They'd be talking to each other like they were at a cocktail party or something. They didn't even pay attention to me. I'd sit up in bed and scream GO AWAY. They'd turn to look at me, with these disappointed faces, and then they'd disappear.

PHYLLIS. Cool dream.

FRANK. Oh come on. It wasn't – please. Don't condescend to me.

PHYLLIS. Excuse me?

JOYCE. Phyllis has a PhD in Psychology. She teaches "Brain and Behavior."

FRANK. I don't see how that's relevant.

PHYLLIS. It sounds like a great dream. What's wrong with me saying that?

FRANK. Ah…I just find it frustrating when people who refuse to acknowledge certain ambiguities in the universe look down on those of us /who –

JOYCE. How many times did you see the, um, the people?

FRANK. They came back every few months. Eventually I realized they weren't going to hurt me.

PHYLLIS. So what are you trying to say? They were ghosts?

FRANK. I'm not trying to say anything.

(A pause.)

PHYLLIS. What's the difference between a ghost and an incredibly realistic hallucination?

(FRANK taps his stomach.)

PHYLLIS. What's that supposed to mean?

FRANK. Your gut. You feel it in your gut.

JARED. *(to FRANK)* You're not being very logical.

FRANK. I don't care for logic.

(after a pause, to JOYCE)

Thank you for dinner. I feel very comfortable here.

JARED. Logic comes from the Greek for the "the art of reason."

FRANK. You're a smart kid, Jared.

JARED. Actually, I'm not a kid. I'm twenty-one. I could have sex with an adult woman.

JOYCE. Jared.

JARED. I could.

(A pause. They all go back to eating. Blackout.)

(JOYCE and PHYLLIS's bedroom. Nighttime. JOYCE is in bed. PHYLLIS is pacing up and down the floor, infuriated.)

PHYLLIS. Okay, so what, some prepubescent girl comes into his studio and takes off her clothes and he's like: I'm going to help you reclaim your body image?

JOYCE. Could you please lower your voice? He's right down the hall.

PHYLLIS. It's totally, it's disgusting, I mean, there are gonna be male college students walking around the Student Union looking at photos of naked prepubescent girls. Oh my god! I'm gonna lose my shit!

JOYCE. It's very very hard for me to have sympathy for you when you haven't even taken the time to look at the photographs.

PHYLLIS. He goes around the country doing this? What a scam. What a pervert! Someone needs to, like, eliminate him from the face of the planet.

JOYCE. Okay. You know I find that kind of talk upsetting.

PHYLLIS. Using art to… oh my god. It's so manipulative. It's so obviously manipulative and *evil.* This guy is like… evil manifest!

JOYCE. What about it is so threatening for you?

PHYLLIS. Threatening? Nothing. I find nothing threatening about it. I find it repulsive and disgusting and exploitative and crazy. I think this guy is like a psycho killer. I think he chops women up and buries them in his backyard!

(JARED *appears in the doorway, holding the Asperger's book.*)

JARED. I have something to say.

PHYLLIS. Jared, how do you feel about a middle-aged man traveling around the country and asking women to take their clothes off?

JOYCE. *(ignoring her)* What do you have to say, sweetheart?

JARED. I know why you guys think I have Asperger's.

(*They look at him.*)

JARED. I've never had sex and you think that's weird.

JOYCE. …I don't think it's weird at *all* that you haven't had sex.

PHYLLIS. I didn't have sex until I was in college.

JARED. You're a lesbian.

PHYLLIS. How does /that –

JOYCE. Listen. It's good to wait. It's good to wait until you're ready, and you've met somebody you really like, /and –

JARED. The book says people with Asperger's have a hard time forging physical and romantic relationships because of their lack of empathy and social prowess and I know that's why you think I have it but you're wrong. I'm just shy, and introverted, and I have better things to do than go to a frat party and get drunk and make out with some stupid girl.

JOYCE. …And I'm proud of you for that, sweetheart.

PHYLLIS. Hold on. Why does the idea of having it upset you so much?

JARED. It upsets me because I don't have it.

PHYLLIS. What makes you so sure?

JARED. I've read most of the book and I've thought about it and I don't have it. And they say there's not a fool-proof test you can do anyway.

PHYLLIS. *(sighing)* Okay. That's true. But Jared? You line up with pretty much every single one of the symptoms.

You have this formal way of talking, you freak out if there's any change in your daily routine, you haven't had a friend in more than –

(JARED *throws the Asperger's book at* PHYLLIS*'s head. She screams and dodges.*)

PHYLLIS. WHAT THE HELL!

(JOYCE *leaps up and grabs* JARED*'s arms.*)

JOYCE. No. No. You cannot do that.

JARED. *(shouting at* PHYLLIS*)* Okay, well, you have Down Syndrome! I read a book on Down Syndrome and I decided that you have it!

PHYLLIS. You can test for Down Syndrome, you little jerk!

JOYCE. PHYLLIS.

JARED. You're stupid and you have no idea how stupid you are and you're like totally oblivious and ugly so I think you have Down Syndrome!

JOYCE. Both of you stop it!

(JOYCE *slides to the floor and sits there, crying.*)

PHYLLIS. *(to* JARED*)* Listen. I'm…a psychology professor is telling you that you most likely have this thing and that maybe you can get help for it. Someone could help you work on your social skills and then maybe you'd actually get a girlfriend and have sex and it could be pretty great, but no, you refuse to go to therapy and you won't admit that maybe, just maybe, you have it! Why are you holding yourself back?

JARED. Because I know. Like that guy Frank was saying. I know it in my gut.

PHYLLIS. I give up.

JARED. I'm going to have sex. Without anyone's help. Just wait and see.

JOYCE. Oh my god. Jared? Do not go out and have sex to prove something to Phyllis.

JARED. You think I have it, too.

JOYCE. …I'm not sure. Okay?

PHYLLIS. Oh, come on, Joyce.

(*JOYCE shoots her a look.*)

JARED. I'm going to get a girlfriend and I'm going to have doggy-style sex with her.

JOYCE. Please. Please don't talk that way. That's not going to make you happy, honey.

(*JARED walks out of the room, then immediately turns around and walks back in.*)

JARED. She's going to be impressed by how much etymology I know.

(*He walks out.* **PHYLLIS** *and* **JOYCE** *look at each other.*)

JOYCE. I am feeling very, very angry at you right now.

PHYLLIS. That's fine. Because I am feeling very angry at you right now.

JOYCE. No you're not. You're feeling angry at Frank Bonitatibus. And you took it out on Jared.

PHYLLIS. (*after a pause*) Were you flirting with him?

JOYCE. Who?

PHYLLIS. Frank Bonifuckhead.

JOYCE. No. Jesus, Phyllis. You have totally lost it.

PHYLLIS. I feel like you were kind of flirting with him. Do you miss male attention or something?

JOYCE. I said no. You're allowed to ask, but then you have to believe me when I say no.

PHYLLIS. Sometimes you can flirt without realizing it.

JOYCE. If I was flirting without realizing it then you have no reason to be mad at me.

PHYLLIS. I beg to differ.

(*JOYCE stands up.*)

JOYCE. I'm turning off the light.

PHYLLIS. I want to read more.

JOYCE. I don't give a shit.

(*JOYCE turns off the light. There's a knock on the door. After a second, the door creaks open.* **FRANK** *is standing in the doorway in a bathrobe.*)

FRANK. Is everything okay?

PHYLLIS. Hunky dory, Frank.

FRANK. I heard Jared yelling.

PHYLLIS. Thanks so much for checking.

(**FRANK** *nods and walks away.* **JOYCE** *and* **PHYLLIS** *lie in the darkness. After a while, daylight comes in through the window.*)

(**PHYLLIS** *gets out of bed, walks over to the blackboard, and writes "Wednesday". She faces the audience and reads the following from an index card:*)

PHYLLIS. Patricia Feinstein began her career as a psychiatrist, but a sabbatical at UC Berkeley in 1975 inspired her to move towards a focus in sexology and sex therapy. Since then, she has worked as a psychologist at Beth Israel Hospital in Boston, a co-director at the Fort Collins Sex and Gender Clinic, and now she's Assistant Professor of Psychiatry at the Cornell School of Medicine.

(**PHYLLIS** *looks up at the audience*)

One thing I really like about Doctor Feinstein is the way she critically examines the modern feminist movement, and the different ways women today are trying to, um, reassert, or, um, reclaim their self-image and sexual identity. Are all of these efforts constructive? Or do some of them just continue our legacy of self-objectification? Take the, um, the new, allegedly "feminist" trend of burlesque dancing. The woman's sexuality is still determined by her onlooker, and to make the, um, common excuse that the dancer *enjoys* exposing and depersonalizing herself is to remain willfully ignorant of the fact that –

(*she suddenly stops and looks into the wings, confused*)

What? Oh. Okay.

We're running out of time.

Sorry about that. Patty Feinstein, everyone. Please give her a warm welcome.

(*She steps out of the light. Blackout.*)

(*JOYCE and* PHYLLIS*'s kitchen.* JARED *is alone, reading the OED at the table.* PHYLLIS *enters with a book. After a pause:*)

PHYLLIS. Are you mad at me?

JARED. No.

PHYLLIS. Because of last night?

JARED. It's not worth my time to be mad. I've got better things to do.

PHYLLIS. I want to apologize for being /so –

JARED. Whatever. I don't care.

(PHYLLIS *sits down at the kitchen table with her book. She glances over at* JARED.)

PHYLLIS. What word are you looking at?

JARED. I'm reading one of the brief introductory essays.

PHYLLIS. Oh yeah? What's it about?

JARED. Prescriptivism versus Descriptivism.

(PHYLLIS *gives him a blank look.*)

JARED. It's like a really really big deal in the dictionary world.

PHYLLIS. Well, I've never heard of it.

(JARED *sighs disgustedly.*)

PHYLLIS. Just tell me, Jared.

JARED. Prescriptivism is the dictionary telling you what the correct definition is. Even if people in the outside world use the word differently.

PHYLLIS. That's what dictionaries are supposed to do, right?

JARED. Well, descriptivism says there shouldn't be any editorial judgment. It says a dictionary should just record what people are saying and writing in the real world, no matter how weird it is. A descriptivist strives to be a Totally Neutral Observer.

PHYLLIS. What are you?

JARED. What?

PHYLLIS. Are you a descriptivist or a prescrip –

JARED. I don't know. The descriptivists have a good point about being anti-ideology, but prescriptivists say that that's not actually possible.

PHYLLIS. *I'm* anti-ideology.

(**JARED** *shrugs.*)

PHYLLIS. ...So you're a prescriptivist?

JARED. I guess. I also just hate people who misuse words.

(**PHYLLIS** *laughs.* **JARED** *continues reading.*)

PHYLLIS. That was funny.

JARED. I was being somewhat ironic.

PHYLLIS. I know.

(**JARED** *puts down the OED.*)

JARED. I have the ability to empathize.

PHYLLIS. Uh-huh.

JARED. I'm very good at empathizing.

PHYLLIS. Well.

JARED. It must be hard to be a lesbian. Right? People make fun of you?

PHYLLIS. Uh. Not that much anymore. Not to my face, at least.

JARED. It must be hard to not be that pretty anymore. To get old.

PHYLLIS. Are you trying to be mean?

JARED. No! I'm telling you that I see how your life is hard.

PHYLLIS. Okay, that's...that's not how you empathize with people. You don't sit there and speculate about random things that might be hard for them.

JARED. What do you do?

PHYLLIS. You listen and you try to see things from their perspective.

JARED. So if you empathized with me maybe you wouldn't think I have Asperger's?

(**PHYLLIS** *sighs and flips through her book.*)

JARED. What're you reading?

PHYLLIS. "Women's Bodies, Women's Wisdom."

JARED. Why are you reading it?

   (after a short pause)

   I'm listening and asking questions.

PHYLLIS. Great.

   (after a pause)

   I have to make the closing speech on Friday. So I'm trying to compile a list of quotes I can use.

JARED. Do you want to use anything from the OED?

PHYLLIS. No. Thanks.

JARED. I hope you're going to provide the audience with concrete information.

PHYLLIS. Definitely. This book has some incredible stories. Like this one woman? She was in her fifties, she'd already gone through menopause, and her daughter was leaving for college. So she started having all these weird empty-nest dreams, like dreams about her daughter being a baby again and nursing, and then she went to the doctor and there were, like, these *cysts* in her breasts.

JARED. Disgusting.

PHYLLIS. Hold on. When the doctor removed the cysts... she found that they were filled with milk!

   (JARED stares at her.)

PHYLLIS. Milk cysts!

JARED. That sounds imaginary.

PHYLLIS. Isn't that amazing?

JARED. It's like a story Frank would tell.

PHYLLIS. *(stiffening)* No it's not.

JARED. Yeah. Like, oh there was a ghost, or like this woman gave birth to a flower or something.

PHYLLIS. It's actually not the same at all.

   (after a pause, touching her eye)

Shoot. Jared. Look at me.

(He looks at her.)

PHYLLIS. Can you see my eye twitching?

JARED. No.

PHYLLIS. The bottom lid? It's sort of jumping around?

JARED. No.

PHYLLIS. Weird.

(after a pause)

Where *is* Frank?

JARED. The Visual Artists' Tea and Reception.

PHYLLIS. Oh god. Just the thought of it makes me sick.

(after a pause)

By the way, I went to see his photographs this morning.

(**JARED** *goes back to reading the OED.*)

PHYLLIS. They were totally offensive and horrible. No surprise.

(No response.)

PHYLLIS. And aesthetically? Not that good. I mean, as aesthetic statements they were just...

(she trails off. a pause.)

I mean, even if they were of men and women both, I still wouldn't like them.

JARED. It's good they're not of men.

PHYLLIS. No. Why do you say that?

JARED. Men are ugly.

PHYLLIS. That's crazy. What are you talking about?

JARED. Penises are ugly.

PHYLLIS. No, no. That's a common misconception. Penises are beautiful.

JARED. You don't really think that.

PHYLLIS. Yes I do.

JARED. But you don't want to have sex with a penis.

PHYLLIS. I can still think they're beautiful.

(after a pause)

Vaginas are kind of weird-looking, too, you know.

JARED. Ew. Gross.

PHYLLIS. What?

*(**JARED** goes back to reading the OED.)*

PHYLLIS. Hey. Don't you ever want to read other stuff? Like a novel or something?

JARED. I need to prepare.

PHYLLIS. For what?

JARED. I told Frank that I wanted to write for the dictionary and he said: "What are you waiting for?" So now I'm preparing to be a lexicographer.

PHYLLIS. How do you prepare to be a lexicographer?

JARED. You read the dictionary.

PHYLLIS. Don't you need a degree?

*(**JARED** looks at her.)*

JARED. I'm an autodidact.

*(**PHYLLIS** looks at her watch.)*

PHYLLIS. It's 3. Don't you have a shift this afternoon?

(He doesn't respond.)

PHYLLIS. Jared?

JARED. I quit.

PHYLLIS. You're kidding me.

JARED. I want to devote all my time to the OED. McDonald's was a distraction. I don't want to be a dilettante.

PHYLLIS. Oh my god.

JARED. Sorry if that pisses you off.

PHYLLIS. Your mom is…are you just expecting that your Mom is going to support you for the rest of your life?

JARED. Just until I become a lexicographer.

PHYLLIS. You need to go back there and tell them you want your job back.

JARED. Too late.

PHYLLIS. I'll go with you. Do you want me to go with you?

JARED. I was also fired.

PHYLLIS. Did you quit or were you fired?

JARED. I knew I wanted to quit but I didn't want you guys to make me go back so I arranged it so they'd fire me.

PHYLLIS. What did you do?

JARED. It's not a big deal.

PHYLLIS. Oh my god.

(**JARED** *goes back to reading the dictionary.*)

PHYLLIS. Your mother is going to freak out, Jared. She is going to *freak out.*

JARED. Yeah, well. I'm hoping she'll empathize.

(*Blackout.*)

(*In front of the blackboard:* **FRANK** *is sitting on a table, eating leftover cheese cubes and drinking from a plastic cup of wine.* **JOYCE** *walks in. He looks up and smiles affably.*)

FRANK. You missed the reception.

JOYCE. Yeah.

FRANK. Want a cheese cube?

JOYCE. I'm lactose intolerant.

FRANK. Okay.

(*he continues munching away. after a pause:*)

Why are you here?

JOYCE. Oh. I. Sorry. I –

FRANK. No. I'm glad you're here. I'm just wondering *why* you're here.

JOYCE. Um. I guess I wanted to see the photographs again.

FRANK. (*gazing at her*) Uh huh.

JOYCE. (*looking around the room*) Phyllis thinks your work is pretty offensive.

FRANK. I got that feeling.

JOYCE. It's funny. The two of us are usually so...on the same page, you know? I mean, we've always prided ourselves on being, I don't know, politically sensitive without being overly P.C.? I don't really like to use the phrase P.C., though, right?

FRANK. I don't mind.

JOYCE. It's just...I think your pictures are really beautiful. And I feel the women come across as very *strong*.

FRANK. So do I.

JOYCE. It's weird to be told you're wrong, you know? That something you think is beautiful is actually –

FRANK. It's okay for the two of you to disagree.

JOYCE. I know.

(*after a pause*)

Hey. Do you ever...would you ever take a picture of *us*?

FRANK. Who's "us"?

JOYCE. Me and Phyllis and Jared. We don't really have any good pictures of the three of...of, um, our family. A family portrait. We'd pay you, of course, /and –

FRANK. I don't let people pay me.

JOYCE. Oh. Then...would you be willing to –

FRANK. That's not really the kind of work I do, Joyce.

JOYCE. Oh.

FRANK. Sorry.

JOYCE. No. No. I was...I was just wondering.

(*after a long pause, trying to sound jokey*)

So you swear you're not a sleazeball?

FRANK. That's a completely crazy question.

JOYCE. Well –

FRANK. What does "sleazeball" even mean?

JOYCE. ... Um. I don't know.

(*she giggles and covers her face with her hands. through her fingers, muffled:*)

Iguesslikeifyoujerkedofftothem?

FRANK. What did you say?

(She uncovers her face.)

JOYCE. Like if you jerked off. If you jerked off to your own photographs.

FRANK. What if I did?

JOYCE. That would be creepy.

FRANK. That would make me a sleazeball?

JOYCE. ...Yeah.

FRANK. That's a very dangerous thing to say, Joyce.

JOYCE. Why?

FRANK. Because then art is all about the intentions of the artist and not the effect that the art has on the audience. Which I think is the more important part.

JOYCE. Oh.

FRANK. I mean, what if Michelangelo masturbated to the statue of David? Does that make him a bad sculptor?

JOYCE. Oh. Sorry. Yeah. I guess I don't know very much about art.

FRANK. I mean at that point you're getting into mind control.

JOYCE. Oh, no, no, I didn't mean –

FRANK. It's just a very dangerous arena.

JOYCE. I'm sorry.

FRANK. Don't be sorry. It's just: do you like the photographs. Do you think they're beautiful.

JOYCE. Definitely. Definitely. But. I mean. Okay. Hypothetically. What if you were like this psycho rapist murderer and you took the pictures right before you raped and killed all these women?

FRANK. You're asking important questions.

JOYCE. But what's the right answer?

FRANK. Do you want to pose for me, Joyce? Alone?

(after a long silence)

I've just been getting that vibe from you.

JOYCE. Um.

(after a pause)

I guess I'm curious about what it would be like.

FRANK. Well, I'm here for the next two days. I have my equipment.

JOYCE. I don't really know *why* I'm curious.

FRANK. It's a tremendous opportunity.

JOYCE. Yeah.

FRANK. It's both a very individual personal thing and an opportunity to become part of something really large and important.

JOYCE. Would you even *want* me to pose for you?

FRANK. What does that mean?

JOYCE. I don't know.

FRANK. I think you're beautiful.

JOYCE. Yeahyeahyeah.

FRANK. I do.

JOYCE. Phyllis would kill me.

FRANK. Why do you think Phyllis is so defensive?

JOYCE. I don't know. Defensive? I mean, yeah. Also protective, I think. She's really protective of me.

FRANK. Why?

JOYCE. Oh. Well. Stuff. I mean, both Phyllis and I have really long histories. I don't know. Um…

FRANK. This is making you uncomfortable.

JOYCE. No. I just think I should…I guess I don't really know *why* I want to pose for you. I don't know if it's, um, for the right reason.

FRANK. Is there such thing as a right reason?

JOYCE. Well. Yeah.

(after a pause)

Yeah. I mean, yeah. I think so.

(He nods. Blackout.)

(JOYCE and PHYLLIS's kitchen. PHYLLIS is sitting at the table reading "Women's Bodies, Women's Wisdom." Her feet are propped up on a chair. She is studiously ignoring JARED and JOYCE, who are standing at the stove. JOYCE is making dinner while JARED hovers behind her.)

JARED. You always said: pursue your dream.

JOYCE. You are not allowed to quit your job and lie around the house reading the dictionary unless you agree to go into therapy.

JARED. I don't need therapy.

JOYCE. Are you happy living like this? Sitting around the house all day? Doing nothing?

JARED. Well, I find most people to be insufferable. My co-workers were imbeciles. And I want to be a lexicographer. Also I'm working on finding a girlfriend. So I'm actually being quite productive.

JOYCE. How are you working on finding on a girlfriend?

JARED. Uh.

(after a pause)

...do you think I could talk to Frank?

JOYCE. Why?

JARED. Because.

JOYCE. Because he's a man?

JARED. I guess.

JOYCE. Oh, sweetie. I'm sorry. I'm sorry your dad's not around.

JARED. I wouldn't want to talk to Dad. He's an imbecile.

JOYCE. I don't know about imbecile. I do think he's a sociopath.

PHYLLIS. *(looking up)* You're going to let Jared talk to that crazy pervert about sex?

JOYCE. I don't think Frank is a crazy pervert.

PHYLLIS. *(to JARED)* I thought you didn't like him. You said he was illogical.

JARED. He is. But he said he's been married twice. So clearly he's had some measure of success with women.

JOYCE. If you want to talk to Frank that's fine. He'll be back later tonight.

PHYLLIS. You're kidding me.

JOYCE. No. I actually think it might be a good idea.

PHYLLIS. Jared, this guy is a real scumbag.

JARED. I just want advice on how to get someone to be my girlfriend.

PHYLLIS. I've had a lot of girlfriends.

JARED. It's different for you.

PHYLLIS. You want some good advice? Ask lots of questions. Pay attention. *Like* yourself. Don't have sex just to have sex. Have sex because there's nothing you'd rather be doing, in that moment.

(*A pause.*)

JARED. I want different advice.

PHYLLIS. Frank Bonitatibus is a loser.

JOYCE. I disagree.

PHYLLIS. And he wants to get in your mother's pants.

JOYCE. He does not want to get in my pants.

JARED. Who would want to get in your pants? You're old.

JOYCE. Frank's older than me, Jared.

PHYLLIS. This is great. Jared is going to get love and sex advice from the guy who single-handedly ruined Body Awareness Week.

JOYCE. What are you talking about?

PHYLLIS. The whole thing is like a joke now. I bring in a nutritionist, I bring in a race and gender panel, I bring in a fucking domestic violence quilt, and then we have exploitative nude photographs of little girls hanging in the Student Union. It's perfect. It's just perfect.

JOYCE. (*to* JARED) I'll talk to him about it tonight.

PHYLLIS. Have the two of you been hanging out a lot?

JOYCE. Stop interrogating me!

PHYLLIS. I'm not interrogating you!

JOYCE. You always do this. You pretend it's out of some kind of cold intellectual curiosity but actually you're just jealous and tyrannical.

PHYLLIS. I am not tyrannical!

JOYCE. Always pretending you know more than me. Like you know my own *thoughts* better than me.

PHYLLIS. Well, sometimes you're just so transparent, Joyce! Your motivations are so unbelievably –

JOYCE. You think I'm transparent?

PHYLLIS. You're /just –

JOYCE. Can you guess what I'm doing on Friday?

PHYLLIS. Um. I don't know. Flirting with straight men? Making organic soup?

(**JOYCE** *gives her an icy stare.*)

JOYCE. I'm posing.

PHYLLIS. What?

JOYCE. I'm posing for a photograph.

(**PHYLLIS** *stares at her.*)

PHYLLIS. You're not. Don't screw with my head.

JOYCE. I might change my mind. But I'm pretty sure I want to do it.

PHYLLIS. Why?

JOYCE. Because it would be freeing.

PHYLLIS. From what?

JOYCE. What?

PHYLLIS. Freeing from what?

JOYCE. I don't know what /you –

PHYLLIS. WHAT WOULD IT FREE YOU FROM?

JOYCE. …Well, my own embarrassment. My own self-consciousness. All that stuff you always talk about. Like being able to look in the mirror? And feel proud? I want to –

PHYLLIS. When I talk about looking in the mirror I'm talking about looking in the mirror *in private.* I'm talking about being able to get away from the male gaze.

Do you get it, Joyce? Are you stupid? THE POINT IS BEING ABLE TO GET AWAY FROM THE FUCKING MALE GAZE! AND YOU'RE WALKING RIGHT INTO IT!

JOYCE. Don't call me stupid.

PHYLLIS. If you pose for Frank Bonitatibus you're an idiot!

JOYCE. God. I just…why do I surround myself with…? The *two* of you. Calling me stupid. Telling me I'm an imbecile. Why is my family…aren't we supposed to support each other?

JARED. I don't care if you pose for Frank Bonitatibus.

JOYCE. Gee, thanks, Jared. I'll just wait until tomorrow when you tell me that I'm stupid for not having read "War and Peace."

JARED. "Crime and Punishment."

PHYLLIS. Okay. Listen. If it's that important to you, the two of us should go buy a Polaroid camera. I'll take as many pictures of you as you want. Sexy naked pictures. You can take pictures of me, too. Okay?

JOYCE. It's not the same.

PHYLLIS. So it…see? It *is* about objectification! You want some old white guy to take the your picture and get a hard-on /from –

JOYCE. The fact that he's white is irrelevant!

PHYLLIS. No. Wrong. It's part of…of COURSE he's white. This is about POWER.

JOYCE. You're not making any sense.

PHYLLIS. If you pose for that man I don't think I can continue being in this relationship.

JARED. Oh boy.

JOYCE. You've got to be joking.

PHYLLIS. I just…I can't imagine it. It makes me sick to my stomach.

JOYCE. You just…are you making an ultimatum, Phil?

PHYLLIS. I'm telling you how it'll make me feel.

JOYCE. And it'll make you feel like you can't be in this anymore?

PHYLLIS. I'm being honest.

JOYCE. Okay…you *know* how destructive you're being.

PHYLLIS. No. No. You are *so* in denial, Joyce. You *have* to know this is all about your dad. You can't admit to yourself that he did something really bad but now you want to strip naked in front of some random sleazy guy and have him take your picture and this just…this is like you compensating for some very, very weird shit!

(After a long, upset silence:)

JARED. Are you guys going to break up?

JOYCE. That would…that would be the dumbest breakup all of time.

PHYLLIS. It's how I feel.

JOYCE. Great. Thanks.

(PHYLLIS goes back to "Women's Bodies, Women's Wisdom.")

JARED. *(to JOYCE)* Can I go play video games now?

JOYCE. Wait a second. What did you do to get yourself fired?

JARED. *(after a pause)* I called someone a retard.

PHYLLIS. That got you fired?

JOYCE. Who did you call a retard?

JARED. The retarded guy who makes the salads.

PHYLLIS. You called the retarded guy a retard?

JARED. Yeah.

(PHYLLIS titters.)

JOYCE. It's not funny.

(PHYLLIS puts her head in her hands and shakes with silent laughter. JARED and JOYCE look at her.)

JARED. If you think about it, I was just telling the truth.

(Blackout. Then moonlight. Then daylight. PHYLLIS walks over to the blackboard. She writes "Thursday". She takes out her microphone. She is tired.)

PHYLLIS. Well, that was incredible. I just…god. I love puppet theater. Those big masks? Um…the whole performance was just addressing so many things, and doing it in such an accessible manner. Thanks to Gary for arranging it.

(after a pause, reluctantly)

Oh. Before you all leave, I'm also supposed to remind everyone to head over to the Student Union and take a look at some of the, um, visual art we have on display this week.

But, ah…well, don't forget, as a sort of interesting exercise, to think about who made each, um, piece of art. It doesn't…it doesn't *invalidate* it, of course, if – for instance – using a hypothetical situation – a white man went to Africa and painted pictures of all the, ah, Bushmen he met there. Not at all. But as a, um, as the viewer, don't forget to think about that. Did a Bushman paint the Bushmen?

Or did a white man?

Okay. Hopefully I'll see you all tomorrow at 3 for the closing ceremony.

Thanks.

(Blackout.)

(JOYCE and PHYLLIS's kitchen. FRANK and JARED sit at the kitchen table with mugs of hot chocolate.)

FRANK. Your mother tells me you threaten to kill her.

JARED. That's an exaggeration.

FRANK. Well, it's unacceptable.

JARED. Why?

FRANK. You know who threatens to kill their mothers?

JARED. Who?

FRANK. Retards.

JARED. I'm not a retard.

FRANK. I know you're not. That thing your mother says you have?

JARED. Asperger's.

FRANK. I don't think you have it.

JARED. I don't.

FRANK. I do think you've been spoiled. I think you've been weakened. No one has ever told you: If You Do That One More Time, Kiddo, I Will Fucking Kill You.

JARED. My mom threatens to take away my video game allowance.

FRANK. That's not enough. But I understand. It must be hard, not having a father.

JARED. It's okay. Will you tell me how to get a girlfriend?

FRANK. You've never had a girlfriend?

JARED. No.

FRANK. You ever ask anyone out?

JARED. No.

FRANK. You ever have sex?

JARED. No.

FRANK. You ever think you're gay?

JARED. No way.

(**JOYCE** *peeps her head in through the door.*)

JOYCE. How's it going in here?

FRANK. Great.

JOYCE. Can I make you guys more hot chocolate?

FRANK. I think we're good.

JOYCE. Okay…

(*She gazes worriedly at* **JARED.**)

JARED. No listening in.

JOYCE. Okay, okay.

(**JOYCE** *darts out.*)

FRANK. So what's stopping you?

JARED. From… ?

FRANK. From asking some girl out on a date.

JARED. I find myself repulsive.

(JOYCE *peeks her head in again.*)

JOYCE. Sorry to interrupt again. Um, Jared? I'm going to Stop & Shop. Do you want me to buy some more of those microwaveable burritos you like?

JARED. Nah. I'm sick of those.

JOYCE. How about the frozen blintzes?

JARED. Those are okay.

JOYCE. All right. How do you feel about spinach /lasa –

(FRANK *clears his throat impatiently.*)

JOYCE. I'm gone, I'm gone.

(JOYCE *leaves.*)

FRANK. You ever help your mother out around the house? With cooking? Cleaning?

JARED. No.

FRANK. You should.

JARED. Sometimes she makes me do the dishes.

FRANK. You should help her with shopping.

JARED. I hate supermarkets.

FRANK. You should go anyway. Ah. Okay! Here's a good starting off point. Life is sometimes about doing things you don't feel like doing.

JARED. Okay.

FRANK. It's also about being confident. You're not repulsive. You're smart. You're self-educated. You've got a lot to share.

JARED. I guess I mean, like...

(*quietly*)

...do you ever look at yourself naked?

FRANK. Sure, sure.

JARED. Is that a weird thing to do?

FRANK. No, no. I mean when you get out of the shower? You kind of...why not, right?

JARED. I just think I look gross.

FRANK. Well. All men look sort of gross.

JARED. Phyllis said men are beautiful.

(**FRANK** *buries his head in his hands.*)

FRANK. Oh Jesus. Listen. You're a straight guy. You're attracted to women. You don't have to find yourself attractive.

JARED. Phyllis said it's important to find yourself attractive.

FRANK. Why is Phyllis giving you love advice? She's a lesbian.

JARED. That's what I said.

FRANK. Lesbians are like…I don't mean this in a bad way. But they're like a different species.

(**JARED** *nods.*)

FRANK. Listen. When it comes to dating, don't be afraid to be aggressive. I mean, don't be a creep. But you can say stuff like: "Hey, I like you." "Hey, I think you're beautiful. Can I buy you dinner?" You can tell women you like them. That's okay.

JARED. How do you know when you can have sex?

FRANK. Well, first try kissing them. If they kiss you back, you can touch their breasts. I mean, this is obvious stuff. If they like that, you can touch their stomach. If they like that, if they squirm around or moan or whatever, then you can start touching their, uh, crotch.

(**JARED** *starts scratching his hair.*)

FRANK. Are you okay?

(**JARED** *nods.*)

FRANK. Do you know about eating women out? Do you know what that is?

JARED. Yeah.

FRANK. I would recommend it. Seriously.

JARED. Okay.

FRANK. If you don't she'll tell her girlfriends and they'll say: "He didn't eat you OUT?"

JARED. Does it taste weird?

FRANK. Depends.

JARED. What if I get grossed out?

FRANK. Don't be a baby.

(after a pause)

I recommend eating the woman out before you actually try intercourse for the first time.

(after a pause)

Also try to focus on acting like a grownup.

(after a pause)

Also don't forget to tell her she looks beautiful.

(JARED *nods.)*

Hey. You look freaked out. Listen. Don't be scared of eating some girl out. That's the easy part. If I were you, I would worry about getting too excited/and –

JARED. Do you think I'm retarded?

FRANK. No. I already said no. Jesus.

JARED. I guess, um…

(quietly)

I guess sometimes I think they're right.

FRANK. You're not retarded. You're living with two women.

JARED. No, but…I mean, it's not…it's not like having Down Syndrome or something. It just means you have a hard time picking up on social cues.

FRANK. So what are you saying? You think you have this thing?

JARED. No. I just…

FRANK. Saying you have it would be taking the easy way out, Jared.

JARED. Yeah?

FRANK. Don't take the easy way out.

(JARED *nods.)*

FRANK. Now give me your toothbrush.

(JARED *freezes.)*

JARED. What. Why.

FRANK. The only thing about you that seems retarded is the fact that you walk around sucking on an electric toothbrush. It's really weird, man.

JARED. I'd rather not.

FRANK. It'll be a symbolic gesture.

(JARED *shakes his head.*)

FRANK. Okay. Fine. Not a symbolic gesture. A, ah…a *necessary action.* If I'm some chick there is no way I'm having sex with some guy who walks around sucking an electric toothbrush.

(FRANK *holds out his hand.* JARED *looks at him. After a few seconds,* JARED *reaches into his pocket and takes out the toothbrush. He puts the toothbrush in* FRANK's *hand.*)

FRANK. My man.

JARED. I find it soothing. I don't see what's wrong with that.

FRANK. It's not sexy.

JARED. I thought men didn't have to be sexy.

FRANK. No, no. We have to be sexy. You misunderstood me. We don't have to be beautiful.

JARED. Oh.

FRANK. You're a good man, Jared.

(JARED *nods. After a pause:*)

JARED. You really can see ghosts?

FRANK. Yep. I see my dead mother everywhere.

(*Blackout.*)

(JOYCE *and* PHYLLIS's *bedroom.* JOYCE *is lying in bed reading. There is a small white line across* JOYCE's *upper lip.* PHYLLIS *enters the bedroom.*)

PHYLLIS. You missed the puppet theater.

(JOYCE *doesn't respond.*)

PHYLLIS. Are you giving me the silent treatment or something?

(No response.)

PHYLLIS. What's on your lip?

(another long pause)

Is that bleach? Oh my god. Are /you –

JOYCE. *(not looking up)* Please get off my case.

PHYLLIS. Why are you *doing* that?

JOYCE. I've bleached my moustache many times before. This is not a new development.

PHYLLIS. But you don't even *have* a moustache.

JOYCE. It just looks like that because I bleach it. I do it when you're not around.

PHYLLIS. You're kidding.

JOYCE. Nope. I knew you'd give me shit.

PHYLLIS. So why are you –

JOYCE. I'm in trouble anyway. You're threatening to break up with me anyway. So why shouldn't I bleach my moustache in front of you while I still have time?

PHYLLIS. You're still doing it?

JOYCE. Doing what?

PHYLLIS. You're still going to strip completely naked for our house-guest?

JOYCE. Yes.

PHYLLIS. Jesus Christ.

JOYCE.	**PHYLLIS.**
And you're not allowed to threaten me anymore.	You're killing my soul!

JOYCE. Oh my god.

PHYLLIS. You're like the one person! The one person I always felt was on my side!

JOYCE. I am on your side.

PHYLLIS. No. You've joined the enemy.

JOYCE. There is no enemy.

PHYLLIS. THERE IS NO ENEMY?

JOYCE. Shhh. Think about it. Who's the enemy?

PHYLLIS. Um, prejudice? Misogyny? Exploitative... exploitativeness?

JOYCE. Those are concepts. Not people. You think I've joined those concepts?

(PHYLLIS stares at her.)

JOYCE. Come on, Phil. You just don't want Frank to take a picture of something that's *yours.*

(PHYLLIS sits down on the bed, dejected. A pause.)

PHYLLIS. Are you attracted to him?

(another pause)

Be honest with me.

JOYCE. ...I don't know. Okay? And that's...that's actually beside the point.

(A silence. PHYLLIS lets out a long, shaky sigh.)

PHYLLIS. My eye is twitching again.

(JOYCE cups PHYLLIS's face in her hands and stares at her.)

JOYCE. I can't see it.

PHYLLIS. *(starting to weep)* It's there! I swear to god!

JOYCE. Okay, okay.

PHYLLIS. I just feel so...

(She starts to cry harder.)

JOYCE. What?

PHYLLIS. Abandoned. Or something. The past four days. I don't know.

JOYCE. Oh Phil.

PHYLLIS. I don't want to give the stupid closing speech tomorrow.

JOYCE. I'll sit in the front row. You can look at me the whole time.

(JOYCE opens her arms. PHYLLIS collapses into them and weeps.)

PHYLLIS. Body Awareness Week has not gone the way I planned.

JOYCE. I know, sweetheart. I know.

(**JOYCE** *reaches over to the lamp and turns it off. Moonlight comes through the window, then daylight.*)

(**PHYLLIS** *gets out of bed and walks over to the blackboard. She writes "Friday". She faces the audience, holding her microphone. She clears her throat, then closes her eyes.*)

PHYLLIS. "If we ever are to create safety in the outside world, we must first create safety for ourselves right in our own brains."

(*She opens her eyes and smiles.*)

I really like that quote.

Safety in our own brains.

First of all. Everyone. Thank you. Thank you for coming, and thank you for participating in, um, whatever fashion you've participated in this week's activities.

I hope that Body Awareness Week has helped to…raise consciousness in some way. In each of us. By consciousness I don't mean self-consciousness, of course. What I mean is, ah…

(*after a pause*)

…Because we want to see ourselves without feeling *seen*. Or, um, I guess, to put it, ah, differently, we want to feel *seen* without feeling *judged*. If that's possible. I'd like to think it is, right?

(**PHYLLIS** *stops and smiles into the front row. She is looking for* **JOYCE**. *She does not see her. She frowns.*)

Sorry. Um…

(**PHYLLIS** *looks out into the audience for a while, then*)

Joyce?

(*She waits. No response.*)

Oh god. Um.

Sorry. I was just…sorry.

Okay.

Ah…

Well. Maybe it isn't possible. Because there's the male gaze, right, and then there's the *white* gaze, and then there's the *white male* gaze…and all of these relate back to the idea of image-ownership, right? Of actually, by looking at something, by observing something, *possessing* it in some way. So if you're like a 19th century painter guy and you've painted this female nude… or if you're a rich guy in the 19th century and you've COMMISSIONED a painter to paint a female nude, and it's like hanging in your, ah, VERANDAH…

(She pauses.)

That's not the right word. Um…

(She reaches up and briefly touches her left eyelid.)

I guess the question is…how do we remain neutral?

How do we observe ourselves, and other people, without participating in the legacy of image-ownership?

I mean, maybe the male gaze is…um …maybe it's not like a spotlight. I've always thought of it as this, ah, evil, moving spotlight…but maybe it's more like, ah… the *sun*. Like it's our solar system and we're revolving around inside of it.

(pause)

But I don't know. I want…I want so badly for there to be a right answer. Because it's just, ah…I mean, I was thinking: if there's no right answer…

Why does the dictionary even exist?

(She is overwhelmed. She reaches up and touches her left eyelid. She stays that way for a while. Eventually she removes her hand and smiles bravely out at the audience.)

For our final, closing performance, I'm thrilled to introduce to you Moonlight and Morning Bird, Vermont's favorite multiracial husband-wife singing duo. They cover everything from klezmer to gospel, and… they're fabulous. They're just really fabulous. Please give them a warm Shirley State welcome.

(Blackout.)

*(***JOYCE*** *is in front of the blackboard, sitting on a stool. She is self-conscious.* ***FRANK*** *is setting up his equipment.)*

JOYCE. When do I take off my clothes?

FRANK. Whenever you want.

(A pause.)

JOYCE. I have a confession.

FRANK. Yeah?

JOYCE. I, uh, I shaved my legs this morning.

FRANK. What's wrong with that?

JOYCE. I shaved my legs because I knew I'd be doing this.

FRANK. I don't understand.

JOYCE. The point of it is, like, this is what real women look like, and I'm gussying myself up? It kind of defeats the point.

FRANK. I really wouldn't worry about it.

JOYCE. I also plucked these little bellybutton hairs I have.

FRANK. Joyce. It's okay.

JOYCE. And I…I trimmed my pubic hair.

FRANK. I think most women probably do that before they pose for me.

JOYCE. But that's BAD, right?

FRANK. Whatever you need to do to make yourself feel beautiful.

JOYCE. But the point is…

*(***FRANK*** *looks at her, bemused.)*

JOYCE. Never mind.

FRANK. Don't beat yourself up about it.

JOYCE. So I get a free print?

FRANK. Yup. I'll send it to you in the mail.

(**JOYCE** *giggles.*)

JOYCE. Am I supposed to hang it up in the living room or something?

FRANK. Some women do.

JOYCE. Oh my god. That's insane.

(*after a pause*)

Sorry. That sounded judgmental.

(**FRANK** *is concentrating on setting up the tripod.*)

FRANK. I'm almost ready.

(*A pause.*)

JOYCE. My heart is beating really fast. I guess I'm nervous.

FRANK. That's typical.

JOYCE. Most women get nervous?

FRANK. Before they take their clothes off. Once they're naked it's pretty exhilarating.

JOYCE. Ah.

(**FRANK** *finishes setting up the tripod.*)

FRANK. I think we're ready.

JOYCE. O-*kay*.

(**JOYCE** *bends down and unlaces her shoe. She takes it off and throws it dramatically onto the ground.*)

JOYCE. Ta-da!

(**FRANK** *nods, unimpressed, his arms folded.* **JOYCE** *bends down to untie the other shoe.* **FRANK** *watches.* **JOYCE** *drops the other shoe to the ground. She looks up at him.*)

JOYCE. Should I take off my socks?

FRANK. It's up to you.

JOYCE. Huh. Okay. Um…I'm gonna leave the socks on.

(**FRANK** *nods impatiently.*)

JOYCE. No! Wait! I'm gonna take them off.

(**JOYCE** *takes her socks off. She begins to unbutton her cardigan.*)

FRANK. You're gonna do great.

(*A pause.* **JOYCE** *toys nervously with the buttons on her cardigan.*)

JOYCE. I have this um…I have this little paunch? I just wanted to prepare you. No matter how much I exercise, I still have this horrible um…

FRANK. Most women your age do.

JOYCE. Yeah. Well.

FRANK. Joyce. I think you're an extremely attractive woman. Please don't get all self-conscious.

JOYCE. Sorry.

FRANK. Don't apologize.

JOYCE. Oh. Yeah. No. I'll just…sorry.

(*She starts unbuttoning her sweater again. She takes a deep breath.*)

JOYCE. Who gives a shit, right?

(*She rips off her sweater, and looks down at herself, in her bra.*)

JOYCE. *(tearfully)* I mean, what's the big fucking deal?

(**JARED** *suddenly walks in. He is soaking wet and shaking.*)

JARED. Mom.

(**JOYCE** *almost falls off her stool.*)

JOYCE. Jared!

(*to* **FRANK**)

Do you have a towel?

FRANK. Ah…no. /Sorry. I –

JOYCE. Sweetie! What happened? Were you *swimming*?

(**JARED** *just clutches his elbows and stares at her, shaking.*)

JOYCE. Jared?

(He doesn't respond.)

JOYCE. Oh my god.

(JOYCE starts drying JARED's body with her sweater. He stands there, passively, letting her touch him. She finally wraps her shirt around his shoulders and embraces him. FRANK watches them.)

JOYCE. Did someone hurt you?

JARED. I won't threaten to kill you anymore.

(JARED buries his face in JOYCE's shoulder.)

JARED. *(muffled)* I did something wrong.

JOYCE. Wait, what?

JARED. I did something wrong.

JOYCE. What did you do?

(JARED suddenly turns to FRANK.)

JARED. Give me back my toothbrush.

FRANK. Sorry?

JARED. GIVE ME BACK MY TOOTHBRUSH IMMEDI-ATELY.

FRANK. It's…I threw it away.

(JARED looks at FRANK for a long time. Eventually he turns to JOYCE.)

JARED. If I don't go to jail, can I go to college?

JOYCE. *(to FRANK)* I'm sorry. I can't do this right now.

FRANK. Don't worry about it.

JARED. *(starting to cry)* I think I'm retarded.

(JOYCE takes his face in her hands.)

JOYCE. You're not retarded.

(Blackout.)

(JOYCE and PHYLLIS's kitchen. JOYCE and JARED sit at the kitchen table. JARED is wrapped in a towel. PHYLLIS is standing at the kitchen counter and microwaving something. A long silence.)

JOYCE. How old was she?

JARED. I don't know.

JOYCE. Okay…how old did she *look?*

JARED. She looked like a Popular Kid.

JOYCE. I don't understand what you were doing there.

JARED. I wanted to meet someone. I wanted to talk to a girl.

JOYCE. So you went to the *pond?*

JARED. First I went to the mall. To the arcade. But there were only guys there. And this one really fat girl.

(**JOYCE** *shakes her head.*)

JARED. Then I remembered how the cool kids used to hang out at the pond. They would go there in the winter and make bonfires.

JOYCE. So she was a high school student?

JARED. Maybe. I don't know.

(after a pause)

How bad is it to show someone your penis?

JOYCE. It's bad.

JARED. Is it illegal?

JOYCE. Yes.

(after a pause)

Did you touch her?

JARED. Uh…

PHYLLIS. Oh shit. You *touched* her?

JARED. No. I was… she was there all alone. She was standing near the water. She said she lived nearby. She was nice. I told her the root of "pond," that it comes from the archaic Old English "pound," and she laughed and said I was funny, and then I just…I showed it to her for like a second. It was literally for like a second.

(a pause)

I was trying to be sexy.

*(The microwave dings. **PHYLLIS** opens it and reaches inside.)*

PHYLLIS. Anyone want a defrosted blintz?

> (JARED *and* JOYCE *both nod, numbly.* PHYLLIS *takes out three plates, puts the blintzes on them, and puts the plates on the table. She gets out forks and hands them to* JARED *and* JOYCE. *She sits down at the table. They all sit, staring at their plates.*)

JOYCE. Did she say anything?

JARED. She screamed and then I ran into the water. When I came out she was gone.

JOYCE. All right. Well. After dinner we'll put in a phone call and let someone know what happened.

PHYLLIS. You want to *report* this?

JOYCE. This girl could be one of my students!

PHYLLIS. Yeah, but how do we know she's going to tell someone?

JOYCE. Phyllis.

PHYLLIS. She might be kind of grossed out but okay, you know? And even if she does tell someone, how're they gonna know it's Jared?

JARED. I have distinctive glasses.

PHYLLIS. I don't know. When I was in grad school this old guy on the subway exposed himself to me and it was disgusting and I was really upset, but I don't know if it would warrant someone like Jared getting in, like, legal trouble.

> (*A pause.*)

JARED. It's just…if I were her? That would kind of be scary.

PHYLLIS. Well, of course it would be *scary*.

JARED. But if someone did that to me…

> (*A long pause.* JARED *is thinking.*)

…I would want that person to…

> (*to* JOYCE)

It's so much better if the person admits to doing it, right? So then you don't have to spend the rest of your life thinking about it.

> (JOYCE *nods.*)

JARED. Also I don't want this to turn into a Raskolnikov-type situation.

JOYCE. What's that?

JARED. Raskolnikov? The main character in Dostoyevsky's "Crime and Punishment"?

(**JOYCE** *looks at him blankly.* **JARED** *shakes his head and sighs in disgust.*)

PHYLLIS. *(quietly)* Do you remember her name?

JARED. L something. Lauren.

JOYCE. Loreen?

JARED. Maybe.

(a pause.)

I'm going to jail.

PHYLLIS. You are not going to jail.

JOYCE. I, um…I don't think I can handle this.

JARED. *(to* **JOYCE***)* It's okay. When I get out of jail I'll get a job at the OED and you can come visit me in England.

(to **PHYLLIS***)*

You were right about needing a degree. I researched it online.

(**JARED** *begins to eat his blintz.* **JOYCE** *and* **PHYLLIS** *watch him in silence for a while.*)

JOYCE. There's a right thing to do in this situation. I just have no idea what it is.

(**JOYCE** *looks miserable.* **JARED** *keeps eating. After a long pause:*)

PHYLLIS. Hey. It's Friday.

JARED. So?

PHYLLIS. It's Shabbas.

(after a pause)

Joyce.

(**JOYCE** *slowly looks up.*)

PHYLLIS. Why don't you get out the candles and grape juice?

JOYCE. Are you trying to make fun of me?

PHYLLIS. No! I'm serious. I think it would be nice. Please?

*(After a long pause, **JOYCE** slowly gets up and gets out a candle and a bottle of grape juice. She pours three glasses. Shakily, she lights the candle.)*

JOYCE. I forget what to do.

JARED. You sing the prayer for wine.

JOYCE. Oh. Um.

(She starts tentatively whisper-singing and approximating Hebrew.)

Baru ama adenoid, emo hey...

*(**JARED** starts laughing.)*

JARED. Adenoid? He did not say adenoid.

JOYCE. Well, I don't remember. Sorry. What am I supposed to say?

PHYLLIS. Um. Here.

*(**PHYLLIS** fishes "Women's Bodies, Women's Wisdom" out of her bag.)*

JOYCE. What is that?

PHYLLIS. "Women's Bodies, Women's Wisdom." I wanted to use part of it in my speech today...but, I, ah...I totally fucked up.

JOYCE. Oh my god.

PHYLLIS. Yeah.

JOYCE. Your speech. I...I completely forgot.

PHYLLIS. It's okay.

(a pause)

JARED. I can have Asperger's and not be retarded, right?

PHYLLIS. Of course.

*(to **JOYCE**)*

Read something out loud. Pretend it's a prayer.

*(She hands **JOYCE** "Women's Bodies, Women's Wisdom." **JOYCE** opens it.)*

JOYCE. Um…

PHYLLIS. Anything.

> (**JOYCE** *opens the book to a random page and starts reading.*)

JOYCE. "Some menopausal women complain of vaginal dryness and thinning, which cause – "

JARED. SOMETHING ELSE.

JOYCE. Okay, okay.

> (**JOYCE** *opens to a different page and starts reading.*)

JOYCE. Um… "*Understanding the Bodymind.* Our entire concept of 'the mind' needs to be expanded considerably. The mind can no longer be thought of as being confined to the brain or to the intellect; it exists in every cell of our bodies."

> (*While* **JOYCE** *is reading,* **JARED** *takes something out of his pocket. It's* **FRANK**'s *recorder.* **JARED** *starts tentatively blowing into it.* **JOYCE** *stops and looks at him.*)

JOYCE. Where did you get that?

> (**JARED** *continues to try out notes.*)

JOYCE. Is that Frank's?

> (**JARED** *nods, still playing.*)

JOYCE. Did you steal it?

> (**JARED** *briefly lifts his mouth off the recorder to speak*)

JARED. He took my toothbrush.

> (**JARED** *goes back to playing. He messily begins to pick out the notes to "Jingle Bells."*)

JOYCE. Oh my god. Jared. What is *wrong* with you?

JARED. I might have Asperger's.

JOYCE. That's not an excuse!

PHYLLIS. It's not a big deal. We'll just give it back to him. He can't be too mad, anyway. I'm about to write him a big check.

JOYCE. Why?

PHYLLIS. I want a copy.

JOYCE. A copy of what?

PHYLLIS. I want a copy of your exploitative nude photograph.

(**JOYCE** *stares at* **PHYLLIS**.)

PHYLLIS. What?

JOYCE. It's just –

PHYLLIS. I thought me saying that would make you happy.

(**JOYCE** *looks like she might cry again.* **PHYLLIS** *reaches over and strokes her hair.*)

PHYLLIS. Why don't you keep reading.

(**JOYCE** *picks up "Women's Bodies, Women's Wisdom" and continues reading out loud. During this next passage,* **JARED** *puts down the recorder and starts ceremoniously waving his hands over the candle's flame.* **FRANK** *appears in the doorway with a suitcase. No one notices him.*)

JOYCE. "Every thought we think has a biochemical equivalent. Every emotion we feel has a biochemical equivalent. One of my colleagues says, 'The mind is the space between the cells.' So when the part of your mind that is your uterus talks to you, through pain or excessive bleeding, are you prepared to listen to it?"

JARED. *(quietly, still waving his hands)* Yes.

(**JOYCE** *puts down the book and watches her son wave his hands over the candle. She is deeply sad. Still unnoticed,* **FRANK** *observes the family for a while, then slowly pulls out his camera and takes their picture. There is a blinding flash of white light.*)

End of play

OTHER TITLES AVAILABLE FROM SAMUEL FRENCH

GUTENBERG! THE MUSICAL!
Scott Brown and Anthony King

2m / Musical Comedy

In this two-man musical spoof, a pair of aspiring playwrights perform a backers' audition for their new project - a big, splashy musical about printing press inventor Johann Gutenberg. With an unending supply of enthusiasm, Bud and Doug sing all the songs and play all the parts in their crass historical epic, with the hope that one of the producers in attendance will give them a Broadway contract – fulfilling their ill-advised dreams.

"A smashing success!"
- *The New York Times*

"Brilliantly realized and side-splitting!
- *New York Magazine*

"There are lots of genuine laughs in Gutenberg!"
- *The New York Post*

OTHER TITLES AVAILABLE FROM SAMUEL FRENCH

FEMININE ENDING
Sarah Treem

Full Length / Dark Comedy / 3m, 2f / Various, Unit set
Amanda, twenty-five, wants to be a great composer. But at the moment, she's living in New York City and writing advertising jingles to pay the rent while her fiancé, Jack pursues his singing career. So when Amanda's mother, Kim, calls one evening from New Hampshire and asks for her help with something she can't discuss over the phone, Amanda is only too happy to leave New York. Once home, Kim reveals that she's leaving Amanda father and needs help packing. Amanda balks and ends up (gently) hitting the postman, who happens to be her first boyfriend. They spend the night together in an apple orchard, where Amanda tries to tell Billy how her life got sidetracked. It has something to do with being a young woman in a profession that only recognizes famous men. Billy acts like he might have the answer, but doesn't. Neither does Amanda's mother. Or, for that matter, her father. *A Feminine Ending* is a gentle, bittersweet comedy about a girl who knows what she wants but not quite how to get it. Her parents are getting divorced, her fiancé is almost famous, her first love reappears, and there's a lot of noise in her head but none of it is music. Until the end.

"Darkly comic. *Feminine Ending* has undeniable wit."
- *The New York Post*

"Appealingly outlandish humor."
- *The New York Times*

"Courageous. The 90-minute piece swerves with nerve and naivete. Sarah Treem has a voice all her own."
- *Newsday*

SAMUELFRENCH.COM

OTHER TITLES AVAILABLE FROM SAMUEL FRENCH

MAURITIUS
Theresa Rebeck

Comedy / 3m, 2f / Interior
Stamp collecting is far more risky than you think. After their mother's death, two estranged half-sisters discover a book of rare stamps that may include the crown jewel for collectors. One sister tries to collect on the windfall, while the other resists for sentimental reasons. In this gripping tale, a seemingly simple sale becomes dangerous when three seedy, high-stakes collectors enter the sisters' world, willing to do anything to claim the rare find as their own.

"(Theresa Rebeck's) belated Broadway bow, the only original play by a woman to have its debut on Broadway this fall."
- Robert Simonson, *The New York Times*

"*Mauritius* caters efficiently to a hunger that Broadway hasn't been gratifying in recent years. That's the corkscrew-twist drama of suspense…she has strewn her script with a multitude of mysteries."
- Ben Brantley, *The New York Times*

"Theresa Rebeck is a slick playwright…Her scenes have a crisp shape, her dialogue pops, her characters swagger through an array of showy emotion, and she knows how to give a plot a cunning twist."
- John Lahr, *The New Yorker*

CPSIA information can be obtained
at www.ICGtesting.com
Printed in the USA
LVOW07s1436240817
546235LV00013B/808/P